How We Met!

adapted by Billy Lopez
based on the screenplay "How It All Began!" written by Billy Lopez and Josh Selig
illustrated by Michael Scanlon, Little Airplane Productions

SIMON SPOTLIGHT/NICKELODEON
New York   London   Toronto   Sydney

Based on the TV series *Wonder Pets!*™ as seen on Nickelodeon™

SIMON SPOTLIGHT/NICKELODEON

An imprint of Simon & Schuster Children's Publishing Division

1230 Avenue of the Americas, New York, New York 10020

© 2010 Viacom International Inc. All rights reserved. NICK JR., *Wonder Pets!*, and all related titles logos, and characters are trademarks of Viacom International Inc. All rights reserved, including the right of reproduction in whole or in part in any form. SIMON SPOTLIGHT and colophon are registered trademarks of Simon & Schuster, Inc.

For information about special discounts for bulk purchases, please contact Simon & Schuster Special Sales at 1-866-506-1949 or business@simonandschuster.com.

Manufactured in the United States 0710 LAK

First Edition 10 9 8 7 6 5 4 3 2 1

ISBN 978-1-4424-0654-4

Did you ever wonder how the Wonder Pets got started? Well, this is that story.

A long time ago, Linny the Guinea Pig was the only animal who lived in the classroom. She liked living there, but she was a little lonely.

One night Linny went to the window and wished on a shooting star. She sang,

"I love my life, you see,
And I'll live it happily,
But I wish I didn't have to be . . . alone."

"I wish I had a friend," said Linny. And just then, she heard a knock at the door!

Linny opened the classroom door and found a tiny turtle lying in a basket. "My name's Linny! What's your name?" asked Linny.

"Turtle Tuck!" said the turtle, and he gave Linny a big hug. From that day on, Tuck lived in the classroom with Linny and they became good friends.

One day, Linny and Tuck found a new cage in the classroom with a funny, round object inside.

"What is it, Linny?" asked Tuck.

"I think it's an egg," said Linny. Just then, the egg started to crack open! "And I think it's about to hatch!" Linny said.

The egg hatched and out popped a little yellow duckling!

"Hello, world! Let's get this party started!" she said.

"Hi! I'm Linny the Guinea Pig and this is Turtle Tuck," said Linny.

"Allow me to introduce myself!" said the duckling and she began to sing.

"The name is Ming-Ming! Ming-Ming Duckling!
The greatest creature that you've ever met!
Behold the marvel that is me,
So full of charm and energy,
And I haven't even grown up yet!"

Ming-Ming began to fly around the room, showing off her wings. But this made Tuck upset.

"That's enough!" said Tuck.

"What's the matter, Tuckster?" asked Ming-Ming.

"It's Tuck! And what's the matter is you're a showoff!" said Tuck.

"I take that as a compliment!" said Ming-Ming.

Tuck and Ming-Ming kept arguing. Linny asked them both to calm down.

"I know you've gotten off to a rough start," Linny said, "but once you get to know each other, I'm sure you'll become good friends. Will you give it a try? For me?"

Tuck and Ming-Ming agreed to give it a try. . . .

... and after a while, they did become friends! One day, they dressed up like superheroes in the fabric scrap box. Suddenly, they heard a voice calling, "Hey! Hey, hey, hey, hey!" They all went to investigate.

Linny, Tuck, and Ming-Ming followed the voice until they found a little rabbit in a cage.

"Hey! I'm Ollie the Bunny!" he said. "Will you free me?"

Linny opened the cage door. Ollie hopped out and started running wild around the classroom!

Linny, Tuck, and Ming-Ming tried to stop Ollie, but it was too late! He hopped inside a toy rocket ship and zipped around the room, out of control.

"For goodness' sakes! How do I hit the brakes?" he yelled, and crashed into a mobile hanging from the ceiling. He was stuck!

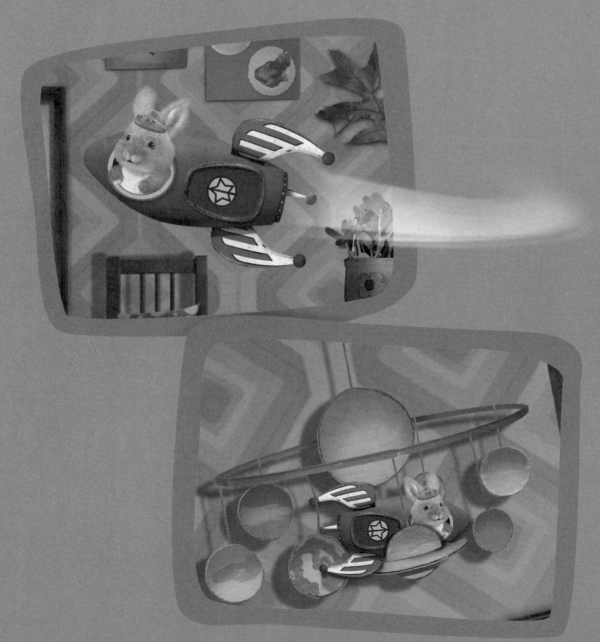

"Whoooooa! I'm slipping!" cried Ollie.

"This is serious!" sang Ming-Ming. Then she added, "Oooh! That's pretty catchy!"

Linny said, "Guys, we can save Ollie if we work together!"

"Yeah!" said Tuck and he sang, *"Teamwork!"*

"Hey, that's pretty catchy too!" said Ming-Ming.

Linny, Tuck, and Ming-Ming all worked together and they managed to rescue Ollie! He thanked them and said they all looked like superheroes dressed in their capes and caps.

That gave Linny an idea! "Guys," she said, "we could really be a team that rescues other animals who need help!"

Ming-Ming and Tuck thought this was a great idea. But Tuck thought they needed a name for their team.

"I wonder what our team could be called . . . ," said Ming-Ming.

"That's it! Wonder!" said Linny. "We'll be the Wonder Pets!"

Just then, they heard a funny sound: RING-RING-RING! RING-RING-RING!

It was a red tin can and it was ringing like a phone! Linny picked up the can and looked inside: It was a baby whale and she was stuck on the beach! The Wonder Pets set off to rescue her!

It took a few tries, but soon Linny invented the perfect vehicle for the Wonder Pets to travel in: a boat that could fly!

"I call it . . . the Boat Fly!" said Linny. Everyone was quiet for a moment.

"Um . . . how about the Flyboat?" asked Ming-Ming.

The Wonder Pets all agreed that sounded better.

They soared out of the classroom and into the sky on their way to rescue the baby whale! While they were traveling, they decided to pass the time by singing a song. The song went like this:

"*Wonder Pets, Wonder Pets, we're on our way!*
To help a baby whale and save the day!
We're not too big, and we're not too tough,
But when we work together we've got the right stuff!
Go, Wonder Pets! Yayyyy!"

The Wonder Pets landed on a beautiful beach in Nova Scotia.

"I see the baby whale!" said Tuck.

"Good eye, Tuck! Let's go and rescue her!" said Linny.

They tried to put the baby whale in the Flyboat, but she was too big!

"This is serious!" sang Ming-Ming.

But then Linny remembered something. "We need to use *teamwork* to save the baby whale!"

"Oh, yeah!" said Tuck. "Just like we did in the classroom!"

The Wonder Pets all worked together to tie the baby whale's tail to the Flyboat and pull her back into the ocean! As they worked, they sang,

   "What's gonna work? Teamwork!
   What's gonna work? Teamwork!"

Soon the baby whale was back in the ocean with her family. Linny pulled out her favorite snack—celery!—and shared it with Ming-Ming and Tuck. Then they all hopped into the Flyboat and flew back to the classroom.

And that's the story of how the Wonder Pets got started!